Dear Parent:

Congratulations! Your child is taking the first steps on an exciting journey. The destination? Independent reading!

STEP INTO READING® will help your child get there. The program offers five steps to reading success. Each step includes fun stories and colorful art. There are also Step into Reading Sticker Books, Step into Reading Math Readers, Step into Reading Write-In Readers, Step into Reading Phonics Readers, and Step into Reading Phonics First Steps! Boxed Sets—a complete literacy program with something for every child.

Learning to Read, Step by Step!

Ready to Read   Preschool–Kindergarten
• big type and easy words • rhyme and rhythm • picture clues
For children who know the alphabet and are eager to begin reading.

Reading with Help   Preschool–Grade 1
• basic vocabulary • short sentences • simple stories
For children who recognize familiar words and sound out new words with help.

Reading on Your Own   Grades 1–3
• engaging characters • easy-to-follow plots • popular topics
For children who are ready to read on their own.

Reading Paragraphs   Grades 2–3
• challenging vocabulary • short paragraphs • exciting stories
For newly independent readers who read simple sentences with confidence.

Ready for Chapters   Grades 2–4
• chapters • longer paragraphs • full-color art
For children who want to take the plunge into chapter books but still like colorful pictures.

STEP INTO READING® is designed to give every child a successful reading experience. The grade levels are only guides. Children can progress through the steps at their own speed, developing confidence in their reading, no matter what their grade.

Remember, a lifetime love of reading starts with a single step!

Thomas the Tank Engine and Friends

A BRITT ALLCROFT COMPANY PRODUCTION

Based on *The Railway Series* by The Rev. W. Awdry

Copyright © Gullane (Thomas) LLC 1993

www.stepintoreading.com

www.thomasthetankengine.com

Educators and librarians, for a variety of teaching tools, visit us at www.randomhouse.com/teachers

Library of Congress Cataloging-in-Publication Data
Thomas and the school trip / illustrated by Owain Bell.
    p.   cm. — (Step into reading. A step 2 book)
"Based on The railway series by the Rev. W. Awdry."
SUMMARY: Attempting to hurry through his work so that he can give some school children a ride, Thomas the Tank Engine must overcome a series of obstacles.
ISBN 0-679-84365-5 (trade) — ISBN 0-679-94365-X (lib. bdg.)
[1. Railroads—Trains—Fiction.   2. School field trips—Fiction.]
I. Bell, Owain, ill.   II. Awdry, W. Railway series.   III. Series: Step into reading. Step 2 book.
PZ7.T36945965   2003   [E]—dc21   2002013409

Printed in the United States of America   40 39 38

STEP INTO READING®

STEP 2

THOMAS
and the
SCHOOL TRIP

Based on *The Railway Series* by the Rev. W. Awdry

Illustrated by Owain Bell

Random House 🏠 New York

It is a big day
in the train yard.
"Let's get ready!"
says Thomas
the Tank Engine.

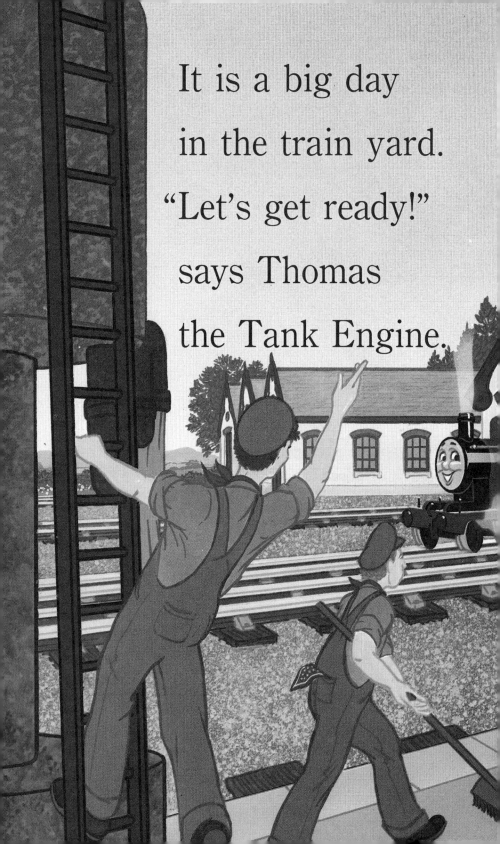

Swish, swish.

The train yard is ready.

Rub, rub.

Scrub, scrub.

The engines are bright
and shiny.

Blue, green, red.

Thomas, Henry, and
James are ready too.

Even Sir Topham Hatt
is ready.

Ready for what?
Children—
on a school trip!
"Peep! Peep!
Here they come!"
shouts Thomas.

"Hello, hello,"
he puffs.
"My name is Thomas.
Watch me push!
Watch me pull!"

Thomas has lots of fun.

But soon Thomas
has to go.
He has work to do
on his branch line.

Poor Thomas.

He is sad.

He wants to stay.

He wants to play.

Sir Topham Hatt
has an idea.
"Do your job, Thomas.
Then hurry back.
You can take
the children home.

"But remember.
You cannot be late.
You must be on time.
Or somebody else
will take the children."

"I will hurry.

I will hurry,"

Thomas says.

His coaches Annie

and Clarabel say,

"We will hurry too."

Chug, chug, chug.
All along his branch line,
Thomas goes as fast
as he can.

Up a hill.
Over a bridge.
Through a tunnel.
Thomas stops
at every station.

At last!

The work is done.

"Right on time.

Right on time,"

chugs Thomas.

"Now hurry back.

Hurry back,"

puff Annie and Clarabel.

But Thomas
cannot hurry.
Thomas has to wait.

And wait.

And wait again.

Oh no!

Will Thomas be late?

Will James or Henry

take the children home?

Oh my!
Now what is that
up ahead?
It is Bertie the Bus.
He has broken down.

Thomas wants to help.

But then he will be late—

much too late.

Stop or go.

Help or hurry.

What should Thomas do?

Screech!

Thomas stops.

He cannot leave

his friend.

"Will you take
my passengers?"
asks Bertie.

Look!
It is the children!
Bertie was taking
them home.

Hooray for Thomas!

He has saved the day!